MONEY LOVES ME

WRITTEN BY
TOYIN ADEKALE

To order additional copies of this book, contact:
Xlibris
844-714-8691
www.Xlibris.com
Orders@Xlibris.com

ISBN:	Softcover	978-1-6698-1059-9
	Hardcover	978-1-6698-1060-5
	EBook	978-1-6698-1061-2

Print information available on the last page

Rev. date: 02/08/2022

FOREWORD

As a child growing up, **Money** was something that always seemed to be a stranger in our home. It seemed we always needed it. Other times we'd have it, and most times we craved it, but whenever we discussed it, it would be for the need of it.

It dawned on me that during my success as a recording artist, I wished for it and got it, but I never really realized I had it until it had gone. Why is this thing called **Money**, so hard to get now? If I had it before, couldn't I get it again, and why didn't I have it for long? All these questions started to flood my mind as I found history repeating itself, in clear view of my children. Then a sudden fear came over me, "I can't afford for them to go through the same belief that **Money** is hard to get and even harder to keep".

I sent my kids a message one cold sunny morning, December 28th, 2016, to be precise. Sitting at my computer, reflecting. I had just gone through a lovely Christmas, but not the way I wanted. It was coming to the end of the year and again **Money** was nowhere to be seen, and if I saw it, it was lean. We had desperate needs that required **Money** to show up immediately; miraculously even. Then it dawned on me....."*Kids we have to talk.*" No it's NOT too late....I don't care if they are young adults. If we don't have that conversation today, when will we have it? Not just my children, but your children, their children....and let's not forget, US. Yes! I'm talking to YOU...Yes you! A teachable adult who is not too old to learn, or at least recognize this. We can then retrace our steps to regain our relationship with MONEY. After all, Money will love us, if we love him back, like any relationship; you get out what you put in.

Let's find **Money**, our long lost love.

Toyin Adekale

Written by Toyin Adekale
Illustration & Animation by Qlogic Entertainment &Techlab Steam

CONTENTS

1
CHAPTER

Money Sneaks Out of the House

My name is Money and I live in a little house on the corner with my keeper Mona, who is a caring, but hard working mother of the twins Loanie and Lendie.

Lendie was so different to his sister Loanie, yet so much alike in that they were always asking questions about Money (that would be me).

One day as I laid on the kitchen countertop, I heard the humans talking about me,
"No you can't take money with you son. Money doesn't grow on trees!"

Mona was yelling at her son Lendie. Yes indeed, it seems I was going to be excluded again. They never seem to see me or care. This makes me so sad. I just wanted to spend time with the humans and mingle with other types of money just like me, but they could never see me right there in front of them. I could do so much with them. Oh well. Maybe I could sneak into Lendie's bag when he's going out. I wonder if there's other Monies out there going through what I'm going through. Surely not all money is treated like this? I feel so lonely sometimes and unloved. You know what, if I don't get out of here, no one will know I'm here to help. I had to make a decision. So I decided to take that step and slipped into Lendie's backpack, unknowing to him of course. I was excited, though a little nervous. What will I discover out there?

As we left the house, I could see the outside world that my ancestors had built, and where some of them lived. There were big beautiful houses, nice cars and stores. I even saw some humans having a good time with all sorts of money. They all looked comfortable with their humans. Some of them were being carried around in beautiful leather attire, called wallets and purses. Most of them were being carried around by grown human adults like Mona, but they weren't just floppy paper or silver and bronze coins; there were some unusual plastic rectangle cards with numbers on them. Some had names on them like Visa, Mastercard and American Express.

Visa seems to be a big family. I saw them everywhere and they were happy too. Even the shops and stores we passed had invitations, saying 'Visa welcomed here'. Humans seem to take them everywhere. In their bags, and in their pockets. It seems to me that when money like me gets older maybe they turn into plastic....wow.

This was a whole new world. So exciting to see, but how do I get to know them and make friends with these other monies?

As we walked along the busy streets past many stores, we came up to a bicycle store. There were all sorts of lovely bikes. As Lendie glared through the window, he saw a beautiful purple bike.

Lendie, put his face closer to the window with a look of excitement on his face. I think he likes the purple bike very much. Lendie pushed open the glass door, with the bell chimes, announcing our arrival as we entered to take a closer look. It shimmered with purple glitter. It had a shiny brass bell and some flashy lights on the back and front. As he looked at the handlebars, his smile slowly turned into a frown. There was a price tag that read $150.00. As I looked at his sad face I couldn't understand why he looked so sad. "*I don't have enough money. How will I ever have enough money for that?*" Lendie muttered to himself.

We left the bike store. I knew there was other money around and we could get together and get this bike. It might take a little time to find my unknown friends, but we could do it. If only he realized.

With that we left the store and continued down the street. What was strange that day was that we suddenly noticed more people riding bikes, not many purple ones, but funny how many people seemed to be riding bikes.

As we headed back home, Lendie continued talking to himself. "*I wonder if I should ask mum to help me get the bike? Then again, maybe not. She never seems to have money*". I was so sad to hear Lendie say this because I knew Mona had other money just like me, but she never let us hang out together long enough. She'd send some of us off to a mortgage company to pay for the house. Some of us went to a car dealership to take care of car payments and others hung out at the bank. But we all came out of her purse. She just didn't keep us for long. I don't think Lendie ever saw a lot of us together so he believed what his mum said. "*I don't have it son. We can't afford it. I've got Bills to take care of.*" Lendie wasn't surprised but still very disappointed as he sulked away to his room. I always hear Mona talk about 'Bills'. He didn't sound very nice but it seemed a lot of her money hung out there. I wanted to find out more about Bills and put him in his place. He caused a lot of sadness to a lot of people as I heard people talk about him a lot.

"*What's wrong?*" Loanie asked her brother, as she lifted her head for a moment from her book. "*Oh nothing,*" Lendie replied. "*That face doesn't say, 'Nothing' Lendie. Besides we're twins, what makes you think you can lie to me...come on whats up?*" Lendie sat on the bed next to his sister, took a deep sigh as he began to tell Loanie about the purple bike he saw and how much he wanted it. "*So how much was it?*" she asked, "*More than we can afford, $150.*" He answered.

"*What?*" Loanie put her book down. "*Are you serious, we'd have to be rich to get that. You know mum can't afford that. You didn't ask her, did you?*" Lendie became even more disappointed with his sister's reaction as now he was absolutely sure that the bike was merely a fantasy, impossible and his sister brought him down to reality with a thud. "*But there must be a way. How do all the other kids have bikes? I saw a lot of them riding their bikes today. How come they can have it and we can't*". Loanie looked him right in the face squarely and firmly and said "*Because they're parents are probably crooks or doing something bad to get that kind of money. Money is not everything Lendie, besides there's important things like Bills to be paid and food on the table and shelter. A bike is not necessary.*" Lendie was no longer disappointed but angry at his sister's reaction. What was she saying to him? That only crooked people had nice things and that they shouldn't want nice things. This didn't make sense to him, or me for that matter. "*I'm going to get a job and get that bike myself.*" He piped back. "*You're too young to get a job*", "*No I'm not.*" "*Yes you are*", "*No I'm not. I can get a job at 12 years old.*". As the twins started to bicker, Mona shouted, "*Will you two, quit arguing and someone come and help me with the chores? There's the trash to be taken out and the leaves to be racked and the clothes to be folded and put away.*"

Loanie was the first on her heels, "*Ok mum, coming.*" She then turned to her brother to have the last say. "*No you can't*!" Lendie sat there for a moment in deep thought, and then his facial expression just changed, as if a light bulb had lit up a new idea. "*I've got it. I know how I can get that bike. I'm going to work for it and I'm going to save. I want that bike, I don't care what Loanie or anyone says*". With that Lendie ran downstairs. "*Hey mum, can I ask you something? Can I do some extra chores for extra pocket money?*" "*Like what son? I can't give you too much, but I guess you can be in charge of clearing out the garage. I've been trying to do that for a while. Maybe you can pack all the books on the shelves into boxes, so we can take them to the charity shop and then you can put all the magazines and newspapers into garbage bags and we'll take them to recycling. That's a good idea son!*" Lendie was excited. "*And how much can you pay me mum? It's going to take me a while so how about $10 per hour?*"

Mona was surprised as she turned to her son and laughed, "*Well how about you don't stretch out the hours and I just give you a flat rate of $30.00?*" Lendie didn't hesitate, "*Deal mum. I'll be finished by tonight. But that is on top of my regular $20 allowance right?.*" And with that he ran to the garage, but not without taking the opportunity to take one last jab at his sister, "*Huh, who said I'm too young to work...hahaha?*" He ran off before she could hit him with her book as she scowled past him.

2
CHAPTER

Is Lendie too Young to Get A Job?

Lendie was tired but energized as he looked around the garage, and observed the space. There was so much space, and so much junk. After clearing it all up, he swept the floor, and called his mother in to look at his great work. "*Wow! Son you did better than I thought*" He had definitely earned his money. With that she gave him the $30.00 as promised. And he was still going to get his $20 allowance at the beginning of the month as they always did. Lendie was elated.

"*Loanie, see I told you I can work.*" Loanie shrugged her shoulders and wasn't too impressed. "*Well it's still not enough for your bike anyway.*" Lendie was about to be upset and then remembered there was another thing he could do to make money. "*I'm going to sell my old comic books.*" "*Why would you sell them, you've had them forever.*" Loanie questioned, "*Yes but I don't read them anymore, I've already read them, they're just a collection now. They must be worth something.*" "*Well seeing as you're the one with money right now, can you lend me some?*" Lendie looked baffled. "*I'm working to get what I want, why don't you do the same?*"

"*I've not got time right now, but I really need this new bag and mum won't get it cos she said I already have a bag, but this one is much nicer.*" "*Well maybe mum's right, Loanie. I mean do you really need this bag and how much is it?*" "*It's not about whether I need it or not, I want that bag. Now are you gonna lend me $10 or not*?" Lendie thought about it and was always happy to help his sister, he agreed, but on one condition. "*Ok Loanie, if I lend you $10.00, how about you pay me back $15.00 when you get your allowance?*" "*Huh! Why on earth would I do that? It's more than you're lending me.*" "*Well it's that or you can wait til you get your allowance from mum.*" "*But it might be gone by then, it's on sale now. It was originally $20.00, but now it's half price.*" "*Well it seems to me that even at $15.00, you're still getting a bargain, it's up to you. Take it or leave it.*" Loanie was irritated. Lendie was absolutely right, even at $15.00 it was still better than $20.00 but she loathed giving him that extra $5. "*Well, I'll just ask mum for it then.*" Loanie knew full well that mum had a rule that you get your allowance on the 1st of the month and it has to last. Once it's done you can't get an advance on it. So she couldn't ask mum to give her some now and the rest later. She'd tried that before. "*Grrrrr....ok then. I'll give you back $15.00 for the $10.00, when I get my allowance.*" Loanie was definitely irritated but couldn't resist the deal as she wanted this bag so badly. With that Lendie put the $10.00 in the palm of her hand but snatched it back, "*Just remember, I need $15.00 on the 1st of the month or I'll tell mum.*" He grinned and gave her the money.

Here I was watching this all play out before me. Lendie was finding more of us, right here under his nose. This was about to get interesting. Lendie then got himself a notebook and decided to keep a track of his money. "*So I earned $30.00 and lent Loanie $10.00, which leaves me with $20.00, but when she gives me the $15 back, I would have made a $5.00 profit and will have $35.00, plus my $20 allowance in a couple of weeks. $55.*"

Wow, his money is already growing. That meant he now only needs $95.00 to get his bike. I was curious, that was still a lot of money; could he really make that much? He was only a 12 year old kid after all and not many kids had that kind of money.

Meanwhile, Loanie had contributed an extra $5.00. That was very clever of Lendie. I thought it was time for me to sneak out with Loanie and see if she had any money friends out there too.

CHAPTER

Does Yen and Loanie Have More Money Than Lendie?

Loanie was the trendy twin. She loved the latest phone or the latest fashion. If her friend Yen had it, she just had to have it too. Infact, whenever you heard them talking on the phone, it would be about their latest purchase.

Mona gave Loanie permission to stay the night with Yen as they were going shopping with her mother in the morning. This was a great opportunity for me to learn more about Loanie and her friend, so I slipped into her backpack for the journey in the morning. This was going to be fun.

The girls woke up excited about their shopping trip. "*Yen, I've gotta get that bag. We can't let our school friends outshine us!*". Loanie's friend, Yen, seemed to be the most popular girl on the block and had it all. Loanie always felt she had to keep up with Yen, even though most of the kids didn't really like her, but she was popular. Of course Yen encouraged her. "***Well I've already got it, so if you want to be popular you'll have to get it too. Oh and look, I've got the shoes to match.***"

Loanie's face dropped. It was already a lot of money; and she already owed her brother and had no allowance for 2 weeks. "*Where did you get these? They're gorgeous, and how much?*" "**Well mum got it from Visa or Mastercard. I think it cost an extra $10** " *Oh wow, really, who and where is Visa and Mastercard?*" Loanie asked. Well of course I now learnt they were the grown up money made of plastic. But I'm sure I heard Mona complain about owing them. "**Ask your mum. I'm sure she's got a money card. Every adult has one. You can get whatever you want and you don't need money to get it.**" Pipped Yen. Well, I was quite surprised. I thought you needed money for everything. "*I've only got $10 to buy the bag, and $5 for snacks and fun. It's not fair. I don't have $20 to get the bag and the shoes. Yen do you think you could lend me $5 from your allowance? I promise I'll pay you back.*" I wish I could shout to Loanie, '**Don't do it!**' But of course, I'm Money, and we all know she can't hear me. What was she thinking? She already owed her brother, Lendie $15 and now she was going to borrow an extra $5.00 from Yen, which means she now owes $20 from her allowance. Or is it about to be more? "**I could lend you but my mother said I can only lend money if I get more back. So if I give you $5 you must give me $8.00 back.**" Well it seems I thought too soon. Loanie was clearly not happy about this. Hopefully she won't borrow the money from Yen. "*What! You're supposed to be my friend. That's more than half of $5. That's not fair! I only needed an extra $5.*" Loanie said angrily. This made no difference to Yen. "**Oh well, I guess you can wait til you get your allowance and get the bag and shoes then.**" Yen knew how much Loanie wanted them, and of course Loanie gave in. "*Ok, ok. I'll give you $8 when I get my allowance.*" Well she's really gone and done it now. But Loanie didn't mind for now, so long as she had her bag and matching shoes, just like Yen, it was worth it.

After a long day out, the girls were excited and exhausted from their shopping trip, and so they headed home. The girls laughed and played, dressing up in their new clothes and showing off to each other. "*Our friends are really going to be jealous when they see us in our expensive clothes,*" Yen nodded in agreement. *"Yes we've got more expensive things than most of our friends. Clearly they're not as rich as us".* Yen added. I was surprised Yen really thought this and even more so, that Loanie agreed with her. How is this possible? Mona always told Loanie she was broke and couldn't afford it. Loanie's bargains that were meant to cost her $20, now cost her $33. This all didn't make sense to me. But what do I know, I'm only Money, but I do know how to count and it seems to me that Loanie has less money because she couldn't wait.

I'd heard enough, and couldn't wait for Mona to come and pick us up and take us home, before Loanie got into more spending problems. Now you may think how can she get into more spending trouble? Well anything is possible.

4
CHAPTER

Money Goes Missing - The Search is On

It was fast coming up to allowance day and Loanie and Lendie are always looking forward to this. Mona calls out to the twins. *"Loanie, Lendie, come on down for your allowance."* *"Coming mum."* *"Coming mum."* Mona always handed the twins their allowance money with this statement. *"Now remember money doesn't grow on trees. Make it last because I don't have any more. I'll be broke by the end of the day, cos I have to pay Bills."* I also felt sad hearing this and I know I'm going to catch up with Bills one day, for taking so much away from this family. Really made me mad. It seemed to bother Lendie too. *"Do you have to say this every single time mum? Why can't you just give us our allowance and let us just say 'Thank You? It always makes me feel guilty for taking the money."* Loanie always took mum's side. *"That's because mum wants us to remember how hard she works for it and so that we are careful how we spend it. You should be grateful instead of complaining.."* But I have to agree with Lendie. He wasn't complaining at all. It can't feel good when someone is giving you something and making you feel guilty for how hard they worked for it. But hey, as I said before, who am I to talk...I'm just Money and they can't hear me. Thank goodness. *"I am grateful. Oh by the way mum, you can give me $15 of Loanie's allowance and give her the remaining $5. She's a fine one to talk about 'careful how we spend it...hahahhah."* Lendie mocked, pulling a face at Loanie, who was not pleased at all. *"But I'll only have $5 for the month and I still have to give Yen $8, so I'll be $3 short and without any money this month. Can't you let me off just this once?."* Loanie pleaded. *"Nope. A deal's a deal. Besides I need every penny of my money and more."* *"Wow Lendie, you're just being mean. How could you treat me like this? I'm your sister, your twin sister, for that matter. I have to give Yen her money or she'll tell everyone at school. You know what she's like.."* Lendie was not going to let this slide at all. *"Why would you borrow more than your allowance in the first place? If you can't pay back, you shouldn't borrow. Now give me my full $15... mum, tell her to give me my money. We had a deal, it's my money."* Mona seemed confused at first, but soon started to make sense of this argument. *"Loanie, what have I told you about borrowing, beyond your allowance? People won't trust you to lend you money if you keep doing this. You'll get a bad reputation as someone people can't trust. You cannot go back on your word. Now I'm giving you your allowance to give your brother what you owe him. You'll have to figure it out with Yen and how you're* *going to get the remaining $8. "* I was glad to see Mona standing her ground and happy she still gave Loanie the money so it was her responsibility to pay Lendie. Loanie gave her brother a snarling look and shoved the $15 into his hands. *"That was very rude of you, Loanie. Your brother did you a favor, that's no way to treat him.* Mona was interrupted by a phone call. *"Hello...yes Loanie's right here Yen, hold on a minute."* Loanie was waving her hand to signal to her mum she wasn't here, but it was too late. Mona handed Loanie the phone. Loanie was normally happy to hear from Yen, but not this time. She quickly put on a happy voice.

"Oh hi Yen, I was going to call you later.....yes I know I owe you $8. I was going to ask you a favor...no I do have your money...ok...no I wouldn't dare not give you back....yes I know your mum said to make sure you get it back....ok I'll bring it round tomorrow....Oh your mum's coming by to pick it up later?." Loanie looked frantically at her mother, pleading for help. Meanwhile, Lendie is shaking his head sarcastically, whilst counting his achievement of $55 in total. *"I'm not helping this time mum, she always makes me out to be the bad guy.."*

It seems Loanie is in real trouble now. As she storms up the stairs, there's a knock at the door. *"Good Afternoon Miss Mona, is Lendie and Loanie home?"* *"Hello Idya, Cashick. Yes, of course. Come in. I think Loanie could do with some company. She's up in her room. Lendie, Loanie, the twins are here to see you."* Mona shouts up the stairs, as Lendie is running down to greet them with a smile.

5
CHAPTER

Cashick and Idya have a plan

Cashick and Idya, were also twins and good friends to Loanie and Lendie. They had just got back from their vacation to the United Kingdom, and couldn't wait to share their adventures. They all go upstairs to Loanie and Lendie's living room, where Loanie is sitting sulking in a corner. *"Hey Loanie. Why the long face?"* Cashick asks as she goes and sits next to her. Lendie couldn't wait to answer on her behalf. *"She's got no allowance for this month, cos she owes money."* Loanie throws a cushion at him. *"Who asked you? It's none of your business. She asked me, not you. And I do have my allowance actually, I just got to pay it out again."* Idya looked at Loanie a bit confused.

"*Er isn't that the same as not having any allowance? I mean if you got to pay it out. How did that happen? More importantly, who do you owe?* Idya was a very detailed and logical twin. Often called Nerdy, but he was very smart. "*You'll never guess who.*" Piped Lendie again. This time they all look at Loanie for the answer. "*Yen*". Well the look on everyone's face, said 'oh no'. Cashick, shook her head in disbelief. " *Why on earth would you borrow from her of all people? She's going to tell the whole school. And I hope you've got her money, cos if not, that's gonna be another problem for you.*" Idya turns to Lendie. "*Wait, you guys get an allowance?* "Loanie looks surprised at Idya's question. "*Doesn't everyone? So you guys don't get an allowance? But you always seem to have pocket money, and lots of it. I was just thinking maybe you can help me out?* Did she really just say that? Isn't she in enough money problems? I'm glad Cashick said absolutely not.

Cashick and Idya explained, they don't get an allowance, they earn their money by doing chores, and get rewarded for good grades at school. Loanie and Lendie seem surprised and Loanie declares, *"I think your parents are mean for not giving you an allowance. But do you get money if you ask?"* *"So, why do you think you should just ask and get what you want?"* Idya asked, irritated. *"If you earn it, you deserve it. Then you'll value it more? Yeah we can ask but it's more fun earning it"* Loanie raised her eyebrows, this wasn't the answer she wanted to hear. Her brother interrupted. *"You guys are so lucky! I wish we could go on holiday to London/England. So what did you bring me?* Lendie jokes". Cashick brings out some funny looking money, which also caught my attention. *"What's that?"* Lendie asks. I want to know too, but of course they can't hear me. Cashick and Idya looked at each other and burst out laughing, *"You haven't seen British Pounds before?"* Cashick's laughter was brief and cut short by her brother's suggestion to get serious. *"You need to figure out how you're going to pay back Yen, Loanie. I think I have an idea."*

Idya always has a money making idea, but this time he was stumped, but suggested making things to sell. *"But you don't understand Idya, her mum is coming over this evening, I've not got enough time, and worst of all I only have $5.00 left. I'm in big trouble. I need another $3 and I'll have to do without an allowance for a whole month."* Loanie began to sob. *"What have I done?"* Well I have to admit, I started to feel sorry for Loanie myself. What had she done indeed? As for Lendie he had no sympathy for her at all. His feelings were she got herself into this, so she will have to jolly well get herself out and he wasn't going to help. Cashick sighed heavily and said,

"I can lend you, but I can't see how or when you're going to be able to pay it back. You have no allowance for a month, and you already have shown me that you're not very good at paying it back. So here's what we can do. I'll lend you $10 under one condition.

Loanie jumped up and hugged Cashick before she had finished talking.

"Ok hold on you haven't heard the plan. I will only give you this $10 but you have to pay me back $18. Now I know you can't do that all in one go, so you can pay me $6 a month for 3 months, until you've paid it all back. A total of $18. If you are late for the payment you have to pay me $1 everyday that you're late on top of the loan." Well this was a genius idea to me, but poor Loanie was horrified. *"What! That's not helping, that's extortion....you're taking advantage of me. Why is everyone being so mean to me? It's not like you can't afford to give it to me. You're just being mean. You're supposed to be my friend."* Loanie was beside herself, pacing up and down, furious with her so-called friend. *"You should count yourself lucky!"* Lendie defended Cashick. *"She's giving you time to pay. She could have asked you to pay it all in one go. Seems to me it's the best deal. You don't have to do it. You could just face Yen and let her know you are terrible with money, and she can let the whole school know!"* Well I couldn't believe what I was hearing but there were lessons to be learnt here for sure; 1.Do not borrow what you can't pay back. It could be very embarrassing for you. I could also see how Cashick always had money. Apparently, she would often help her friends out with money and charge them extra, then they could pay her back over time. This was a brilliant idea for Cashick not so for Loanie, but she had no choice. The deal was done, Yen's mum picked up the money and Loanie saved herself from embarrassment.

6
CHAPTER

Money Catches Up With Bills

This was the day I had been waiting for. This was the day I get to face Bills and find out why they were stressing Mona every month around the same time, for as long as I can remember. Not just Mona but I heard other people come around and never had anything good to say about Bills, other than they were going to pay them. Well I have to figure out how to put a stop to this, so, as you guessed, I popped into Mona's bag as she set off to pay Bills.

One thing I love about hanging out with Mona, she's always talking to herself. Makes me feel almost human, as if she's talking to me, but clearly she's not. Mona mumbled to herself, as she got into her very nice car. "*Right, first I have to go to the bank and cash this check and, I must remember to pop into the car dealers to make a payment. I know it's easier online, but I don't want anyone stealing my money. I like good old fashioned face to face payments.*" Sounds like she is trying to convince herself that this was the best way, but I'm not convinced at all. It seems like a rather long way around doing things.

Our first stop was to the nearest gas station. *"Oh dear, I'm low on gas, but this station is way too expensive. I'm not paying that much for gas."* Mona sounded rather irritated at the price. *"I'm sure it's 5 cents cheaper down the road. I'm going there instead."* And with that she drove out of this gas station and onto another, which wasn't much cheaper at all. In fact it cost more. And so again we drive off to another. Three gas stations later and indeed 5 cents cheaper than the first, Mona finally gets her gas. I wondered to myself had she saved anything at all? But who am I? I'm only Money, what do I know? Mona used her plastic card to pay, grumbling and complaining through the whole process. Her card was called Visa, and to my surprise she uttered, *"Oh and I must remember to pay my Credit Card Bills."* This was confusing to me but I'm hoping by the end of my trip with Mona, all will be clear.

Our next stop is the bank. As Mona made her way to the counter, she pulled out a piece of paper called a check. I'd never seen this before, but the lady over the counter knew exactly what it was. *"Hello Ms Poorpus, payday check?"* She says with a smile as Mona greets her back with a half smile. Mona requested cash for the check. The clerk happily asks her, *"Hope you're going to treat yourself to something nice from your paycheck?"* Mona sighs and says, *"No, it's all going to Bills. I can't afford to treat myself right now!"*

The clerk was very encouraging and told her that she should at least spend a little on herself, but Mona shook her head, "*I'm afraid not for a while. Anyway can you also put $200 towards my credit card bill?*" The clerk nodded, "*Of course I can.*" and took the $200, gave Mona a receipt and the rest of her cash. Mona explained,

"*I've done quite a lot of spending on my credit card. I bought a new TV for the house, and I paid for the light bill, insurance and did extra groceries this week, as we were having guests. Not to mention the cost of gas right now! I just filled my car with gas and it was so expensive. It's a good thing I have the credit card to borrow a little extra money, or I wouldn't be able to cope. All I do is spend, spend, spend!*"

So wait a minute, I get it now. The credit card is like borrowing money, and Bills isn't a person, it's the name for the cost of things....wow. I know my name is Money and I should know better, but all this time I thought Bills was a mean, money grabbing villain, when all along Bills takes care of everything. I mean if she didn't have a car, she wouldn't have Bills, If she didn't have the TV or the house, she wouldn't have Bills. You mean we actually need Bills? Well you could blow me down with a feather, I just couldn't believe how humans had made Bills out to be so bad. He comes with everything they want or need. Why wouldn't they pay Bills happily? Especially credit card Bills, because the credit card is money they borrowed! Wow! To think I thought it was all her money. It was a relief finding out that Bills is in more places than one and is not such a bad thing after all. I also discovered that even rich people have Bills.

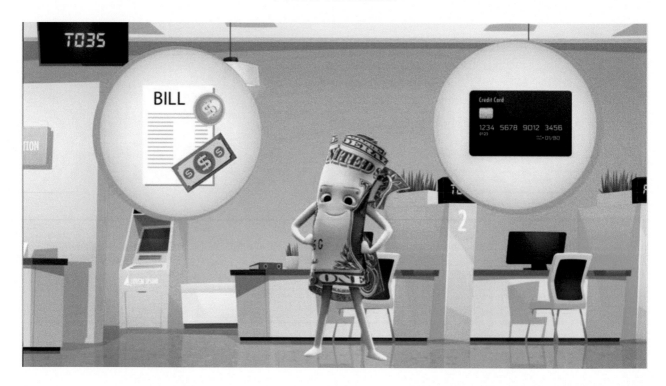

I couldn't wait to get back to the house. Not only do I owe Bills an apology, but I have to find a way to get Mona, Loanie and Lendie to stop being so mad at Bills. Bills is the friend that keeps their electricity on, their telephones on and a roof over their head. The clothes that they wear. You sometimes have a choice of what Bills you want or don't want. And it's the reason Mona goes to work so they can have a better life.

Now all they need to figure out is how to save some of their money so that it grows. Then they will have more money, to do other things, like treat themselves. I wonder if they'll figure it out.

Mona's Delight - Money Grows Where Money Goes

Lendie had been busy doing odd jobs around the neighborhood and saving his allowance. As he pulled out his box from under his bed, sat down and began counting the contents, a big smile stretched across his face. *"100, 110, 120, 130, 140...I did it, I did it."* Lendie jumped up with excitement. *"Mum, I did it, I've almost raised the money for my bike. Well I just need $10.00 to make it $150. Can I do something to earn it mum and can you go with me to get it? Please, please, please"* Lendie's excitement caught the attention of his sister, who came to see what the excitement was about. *"Where did you get all that money from?"* Loanie asked, with her eyes wide open in amazement.

"I worked for it and saved my allowance. I had to do without a few things but it was worth it. Now I can finally get my bike if mum would just help me with the last $10. Can you mum?" Mona looked just as surprised as Loanie, but she was aware that he was saving and working really hard to make money. *"I have to say I'm really impressed with your determination, Lendie. We could certainly learn from you. You did go without treats and games that you would normally spend your allowance on, and you've certainly been very helpful with the extra chores around the house."*

"Wait! You're not going to just give it to him are you mum?" Loanie stated her objection. *"You wouldn't give me the money to pay back Yen, so why are you giving Lendie $10? That's not fair!"* Mona waved the twins to take a seat on the sofa, beside her, so she could talk to them. *"Come and take a seat both of you. I need to apologize to you both and Loanie, you need to really listen to this. Your brother has really taught us both something here, if you care to listen."* As they both sat down, Loanie folded her arms with a grumpy expression on her face, but gave mum her attention. *"I have to say, I've not been a great example to you both about Money. Loanie, let me explain why I am going to give your brother the $10. He saw something he wanted and didn't expect me just to get it for him. He worked for it and saved what money he made. He also put his allowance to good use. He didn't borrow from anyone or put himself in an embarrassing situation. Loanie I couldn't give you the money even if I wanted to, because you just kept borrowing first from your brother and then from Yen and then from Cashick. How were you ever going to pay anyone back if you just kept borrowing from everyone. Besides you would have had a bad falling out with Yen had Cashick not saved you. So you see we have something to learn here. If you really want something, you have to be prepared to work for it, and that might mean having to miss a treat or two, or having to miss going out or buying something you don't need, to impress your friends. Don't be mad about it, but learn from it. I have learnt and from now on, I will stop telling you both I can't afford things. Instead we'll figure out how to save or work for what we want."* Mona hugged the children and Loanie relaxed

her frown and shook her head to show her mother she understood. *"Ok mum"*, Loanie turned to her brother Lendie, *"You know Lendie, I am grateful and I'm sorry I was so mean to you. You were right not to lend me the money, and even better you taught me what to do next time I want something."* *"That's ok Loanie, I just knew there had to be a better way and to be honest, saving my money was more fun than difficult. The more it grew, the more I wanted to save."* Mona got up, clapped her hands together and summoned the twins. *"Come on guys let's go get that bike, and how about we grab a take away on our way back to celebrate?"*

Of course I'm Money, I don't eat, and I couldn't show them how excited I was, but I can certainly tell you I was so excited. I couldn't believe what I was hearing, Mona must have read my mind. This was the best day for me as I got to hang out in the box with Lendie's money before they left for the bike store. We chatted and laughed and they promised me that they were going to venture to another home, purse or bank and hang out to make someone else's dreams come true.

Start a little savings today because my money friends will grow for you too.

THE END

DISCUSSION

1. Do you think children should have an allowance and why?

2. What other ways can children make money?

3. What do you think about the way Lendie treated his sister?

4. What did you learn about Loanie and Yen's friendship?

5. What do you think when you see people wearing expensive clothes, and a nice car?

6. Do you have to give all your money to bills or can you save and pay bills at the same time? Explain your answer.

7. Name 3 good ways to make money and save money in the next 3 months. Make a plan.

CREDITS

I thank God for the revelation and gifts bestowed upon me. The download of information has been an awakening lesson to me. Thank you for the provisions to bring this lesson to the masses.

Thank you to my children Talitha and Bakari, (who sadly left us before this book was completed), for the inspiration for this book. And Talitha for your valuable input and feedback.

Thank you to my friends, for your honest feedback and proofreading, Keziah Job, Sandra Haynes and Patrick Walsh.

And last but certainly not least, thank you so much to Jake for bringing this amazing team together for the illustrations, animation and illuminating this project to the next level. Jazzy, Fizy and Jake, otherwise known as Qlogic Entertainment and Techlab Steam and the team, your belief in this project and jumping on has been so encouraging. I really cannot thank you enough. I've learnt so much and am grateful for your support in realizing my dream. Bless you guys...truly grateful.

For all of us, may Money loves us, let's take care of it, so that it takes care of us too.

Yours literally,
Toyin Adekale

Printed in the United States
by Baker & Taylor Publisher Services